June 28, 1983
For Rosemary Courtney,
with pleasure!
Nonny Hogrogian
David Kherdian

RIGHT NOW

BY DAVID KHERDIAN
& NONNY HOGROGIAN

ALFRED A. KNOPF, NEW YORK

THIS IS A BORZOI BOOK
PUBLISHED BY ALFRED A. KNOPF, INC.
Text Copyright © 1983 by David Kherdian
Illustrations Copyright © 1983 by Nonny H. Kherdian
All rights reserved under International and Pan-American
Copyright Conventions. Published in the United States by
Alfred A. Knopf, Inc., New York, and simultaneously
in Canada by Random House of Canada
Limited, Toronto. Distributed by
Random House, Inc., New York.
Manufactured in the United States of America
0 2 4 6 8 9 7 5 3 1
First Edition

Library of Congress Cataloging in Publication Data
Kherdian, David. Right now. Summary: A child considers
a range of daily experiences—happy, disappointing, painful,
dismaying, and mostly, hopeful—and emphasizes
that the most important one is
what is happening "right now."
I. Hogrogian, Nonny, ill. II. Title.
PZ7.K527Ri 1983   [E]   82-21185
ISBN 0-394-85596-5   ISBN 0-394-95596-X (lib. bdg.)

RIGHT NOW

Yesterday a daisy died.

But right now a whole field is blooming,
and butterflies are everywhere,
and hummingbirds and caterpillars,
and everything is singing its own kind of song,
and I am singing too.

Tomorrow I'm going to the zoo.
To see the elephant, to see the zebra,
to see the lion, to see the leopard,
to see the lizard, to see the water buffalo,
the bear and the wildebeests.

But right now the rain is falling
on everything, including me.

Yesterday I lost my shoe in the pond.
I couldn't catch it, I couldn't reach it,
I couldn't find a friend to help me.

But right now I'm running through the meadow.

Last night my brother hit me,
my mother scolded me,
my father sent me to bed,
and my sister wouldn't talk to me.

But right now we're weeding
in our garden.

Yesterday Jessie chased Sossi
and we couldn't find her anywhere.
We looked in the tree, we looked
under the porch, we looked on the roof,
we looked under the bushel basket.

But right now Sossi's licking milk as usual.

Last week I went looking for a porcupine.
I couldn't see one, I couldn't smell one,
I couldn't hear one, and I never even
saw a track.

But right now I'm coloring in my new book.

My mother wouldn't let me help her with
the cherry pie.

But right now the cakes we are making smell
so deliciously muddy, feel so gummy-gooey,
look so real and perfect
that I can't wait to make mud cookies too.

Next year I'll have a new teacher,
and maybe I'll like her and maybe I won't.
And I'll learn to sing and draw and read,
and have homework and school books
like everyone else.

But right now
I'm swinging in the apple tree.

This morning I had a fight with Janey.
We screamed at each other and cried,
and said we'd never play again
and went home and told our mommies.

But right now Janey's my best friend
in the whole world.

A little while ago I fell off my bike
and scraped my ankle, and skinned my knee,
and bumped my elbow, and hurt my side.

But right now I can feel my knee tingle.

Pretty soon my mother is going to buy me
a new winter coat.

But right now the geese are flying overhead,
the leaves are turning colors,
and the apples are ripe and delicious.

Tomorrow morning the sun will wake me.

But right now the stars are twinkling Hello,
the moon is saying Good Night,
the covers are warm and cozy,
and my sister is snoring as usual.

Sometimes I wish I could fly like a bird,
but right now I like just being me.